Walter Cianciusi

EVENT SCORES

2002-2007

Lulu Enterprises

EVENT SCORES

2002-2007

ISBN 978-1-84753-568-9

Published by

Lulu Enterprises, Inc.

860 Aviation Parkway, Suite 300

Morrisville, NC 27560

Tel: (919) 459-5858

Fax: (919) 459-5867

www.lulu.com

a Daniela

Bruna

Alice

Bettina

Orazio e Camilla

Music For Mobile Phone No. 1

Replace the battery.

2002

Music For Mobile Phone No. 5

Hide the phone in the shadows of a
crowded concert hall.
During the show call the hidden
phone from another one and...
wait silently for audible reaction
from audience.

2002

Lilo

Little girl: “Aloha!”

2002

Music For Eric Andersen

Hear in the now frontier.

2002

Three Internet Events

Subscribe.

Download.

Unsubscribe.

2002

Britney Spears
(Twenty Times)

Listen to the song
"...Baby One More Time" 20 times,
changing every time the settings of
your equalizer.

2002

Music For Guitar

1. Fill the body with picks.

2. Shake!

2002

Computer Music

Defragmenting Drive C:

2002

PlayStation® Event

Reset before winning.

2002

Music For Roger Reynolds

Eat different kinds of ice creams
listening to the Allegro from
the Beethoven's "Emperor"
Concerto for Piano and Orchestra.

2002

Eating Instructions

1. Take an Oreo biscuit.

2. Twist it.

3. Lick the cream.

4. Now dunk it in the milk...

5. and ummm...!

2002

Fluxlist Fun Piece #8

Ride BMX.

2002

Guitar Boom

1. Place the guitar on a prop.

2. Light some firecrackers.

3. Insert the firecrackers in the guitar's hole.

4. Boom !

2002

Dumb Computer

Remove the sound card
from your PC.

2003

Sonata

Allegro

Andante

Allegretto

Allegro

2003

Disembodiment

breast-feeding
(only if the performer is female)

crying

cutting the coat/hair

cutting the nails

defecating

ejaculating
(only if the performer is male)

menstruating
(only if the performer is female)

removing the earwax

removing the eye-rheum

removing the snot

spitting

sweating

urinating

vomiting

2003

Musica Sottolio (Music In Oil)

A musical instrument in oil.

2004

Musica Sottaceto (Pickled Music)

A musical instrument in vinegar.

2004

Composition #65

The "beep" polyphony at the cash desks of a supermarket.

2005

Composition #66

Longitude x

Latitude y

Time z

2005

Composition #67

A music coming from a speaker
buried in the sand.

2005

Composition #68

While watching an orchestra
playing on TV
turn down the volume and listen to
environmental sounds.

2005

Installation

A PlayStation® torn by a bullet.

2004

Installation

Books on the spit.

2004

Installation

Paintings on the reverse side.

2005

Installation

Big pencil sharpener, little pencil.

2005

D.C.

Count the years starting from the birth of John Cage.

2005

Untitled

A famous melody transcribed as a standard MIDI file.
A different General MIDI timbre/instrument is applied to each sound.

2006

Peacemaker

Out = 1 - In

2006

Tired Music for piano

The player produces a cluster
falling to the keyboard.

2006

Tired Music II for piano

Volunteers from audience,
in single file, wait the turn
to place the bottom
on the keyboard of a piano
producing a cluster.

2006

Installation

A windscreen wiper
working on a TV screen.

2006

Instant Painting

A sheet of absorbing paper
on a wet surface.

2006

Installation

A Christmas ~~tree~~ cactus.

2007

Nail Music

Fingernail on sandpaper.

2003

Usque Ad Sidera

A handful of Mentos candies
into a bottle of Diet Coke.

2007

Musica Coatta (Forced Music)

Normalize to 1%.

2003

Musica Inaudita V

for triangle

The triangle part from the
"Piano Concerto No. 1 in E flat"
by Franz Liszt.

2005

Musica Stracciata
(Torn Music)

Fragments from scores.

2003-present

Mind The Gap
for two or more performers
from the New York
Miniaturist Ensemble

During a concert the musicians
replay an already performed
composition standing as far as
possible from one another
(according to the dimensions
of the concert room).

2006

FluxFraud

1. Learn to reproduce the signature of your favourite artists.
2. Start a business on ebay.

2007

Sound Installation

A bunch of carabiners hung on the face of a high and windy mountain.

2007

Unum Scio

Do not speak
for the rest of your life.

2007

Dialogue

Reply to any question with
a single word: “yes” or “no”.

2007

Installation

A dead fish.

A green apple.

2007

Drone Music

Lighters.

2007

FluxDiet

Drink if you want to eat.
Eat if you want to drink.

2007

Untitled

Gently wiping the dust from books.

2007

Concert Bass Drum

1 Hz, mezzo forte.

2007

Untitled

A collection of rear-view mirrors.

2007

Drone Music

Destroy a beehive.

2007

FluxPresent

Gift paper + Ribbon

2007

CONTENTS

CONTENTS

CONTENTS

CONTENTS

www.ingramcontent.com/pod-product-compliance
Ingram Content Group UK Ltd.
Pitfield, Milton Keynes, MK11 3LW, UK
UKHW041914190726
13854UKWH00003B/1245

9 781847 535689